Two Kittens Come Home

A Two Kittens Book

Written by Carlo A. DeMaio

Illustrated by Luis Lopez

© 2018 Carlo A. DeMaio d.b.a. DaRad Publishing
Illustrations by Luis Lopez

Edited by Nicole Bertrand www.nicolebertrandphotography.com

***Every day is a new day to dream
bigger and happier.***

For my children.

*Thanks to my parents and sisters,
Tracy, Laurel, Nicole, Eva and so
many friends who have been with
me on my journey.*

"Lily, Luke," Dad called out, "I have a surprise for you! Aunt Laura's cat just had kittens and they need a new home. We're going to adopt two, one for each of you. We'll go visit Aunt Laura this weekend so each of you can pick one out."

The next Saturday was a sunny afternoon and they went to visit the new kittens. Luke and Lily walked into Aunt Laura's backyard and found seven kittens playing in the grass. They were all different colors —yellow with black stripes, black with yellow stripes, grey with black and white stripes, and one that was completely black.

It was going to be a difficult task to pick just one kitten. Lily and Luke wanted to bring them all home, but they could only pick one each. "That was the agreement," Dad reminded them, "one each."

Lily and Luke sat there and looked at the kittens, some were bigger and some were smaller, they just couldn't make up their minds! They played with the kittens, hugged them and petted them. They were all so loveable, but they could only pick one each and no more.

After some more playing, the smallest kitten, grey with black and white stripes, snuggled up to Lily, climbed on her lap, and started purring. The kitty's eyes slowly closed and she fell asleep. Lily decided right then that this kitten would be her special kitten.

Almost at the same time, Luke decided that the black kitten would come home with him. He loved the black kitten because she was different from the rest and was having fun playing with Luke as he dangled a string in front of her.

And, so it was decided! Lily and Luke

had two new kittens to call their own. The

only problem is that they would have to

wait three weeks before the kittens could

come home with them. The new kittens

needed to stay with their mommy until

they were ready for their new home.

It was going to be very hard to wait, but both kids understood that the kittens needed to be with their mommy just a little bit longer. While they waited, Lily and Luke asked Dad to help them get the house ready for the kittens. Lily, Luke and Dad spent the next few weeks searching for a perfect place for the kittens to sleep and eat, a place for the litter box, and a place to keep all of the kitty toys.

All of this planning was a lot of work, but it was important that the kittens were comfortable in their new home.

Now, after 3 weeks of careful planning and a lot of waiting patiently, the day was here. "Luke!, I'm not dreaming! This is really the day!" Lily exclaimed. They were so excited that they were jumping on the couch.

Lily and Luke kept looking out the window and when they saw Aunt Laura's minivan turn the corner they both shouted, 'They're here! They're here!" in the loudest voices they had.

Aunt Laura got out of the minivan holding a basket.

She was holding the basket very carefully with two hands and was talking to it. And, while the kids were always happy to see Aunt Laura, there was an even bigger reason for all of the excitement.

The basket, or more importantly, what was in the basket, was the reason for all of the excitement.

"I can't believe we are really getting kittens! I'm soooooooo happy!" Lily said. The basket had 2 tiny kittens nestled in it. One kitten for Lily and one kitten for Luke.

Be sure to follow the series to see what's next when the Two Kittens explore their new home.

Subscribe online at www.carlodemaio.com/author for updates and you'll receive FREE COLORING PAGES from the story.

Help bring the joy of the Two Kittens Books to other readers, please leave your **review on Amazon**.

About the Author:

CARLO A. DEMAIO is a debut children's book author. After attaining his MBA in finance and enjoying a successful career in business, Carlo obtained his Masters of Arts in Teaching and decided to pursue a lifelong dream of writing a children's book. Carlo's core inspiration are his two phenomenal children, who keep him young at heart, and his family, where he grew up the youngest of 5 in a first-generation Italian American family, who taught him the importance of education, diversity, and charity. He lives in Fairfield, CT where he likes to new tinker with technology in his spare time.

About the Illustrator:

Luis Felipe Lopez is an artist who specializes in commissioned artwork, including portraits, illustrations and sculptures. Luis' work style includes watercolor, acrylics, photography and digital renderings. He is a native of Black Rock CT, a graduate of Bullard Havens Technical High School, and is currently enrolled at Norwalk Community College studying Graphic Design and Painting.

Made in the USA
Lexington, KY
08 July 2018